This book belongs to:

. . . .

OXFORD
UNIVERSITY PRESS

Great Clarendon Street, Oxford OX2 6DP

Oxford University Press is a department of the University of Oxford.
It furthers the University's objective of excellence in research, scholarship,
and education by publishing worldwide in

Oxford   New York

Auckland   Cape Town   Dar es Salaam   Hong Kong   Karachi
Kuala Lumpur   Madrid   Melbourne   Mexico City   Nairobi
New Delhi   Shanghai   Taipei   Toronto

With offices in
Argentina   Austria   Brazil   Chile   Czech Republic   France   Greece
Guatemala   Hungary   Italy   Japan   Poland   Portugal   Singapore
South Korea   Switzerland   Thailand   Turkey   Ukraine   Vietnam

Oxford is a registered trade mark of Oxford University Press
in the UK and in certain other countries

British Library Cataloguing in Publication Data
Data available

ISBN: 978-0-19-272914-9 (paperback)

1 3 5 7 9 10 8 6 4 2

Printed in China

Paper used in the production of this book is a natural,
recyclable product made from wood grown in sustainable forests.
The manufacturing process conforms to the environmental
regulations of the country of origin

Wobble Bear Gets Busy

Ian Whybrow & Caroline Jayne Church

OXFORD
UNIVERSITY PRESS

This is the way
that some bears crawl.

What about . . .

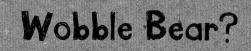

Wobble Bear?

No! Not at all!

Wobble Bear has learned to walk,
so everywhere he goes,
he likes to wibble-wobble
on his wibbly wobbly toes.

Early in the morning,
he goes to Mummy's room,
tries Mummy's shoes on
boom, boom, boom!

'Far too early,' Mum yawns.
'Go back to bed!'

Wobble Bear walks on
his daddy instead.

Down the stairs to breakfast.

Whose tail is that?

Look out, Wobble's about!

'Miaow!'
goes
the cat.

'What a quick eater!
Where's that breakfast gone?'
Wobble's in a hurry now
to turn the music on.

Look at
Wobble dancing,
round
and round
and round.

Now he's feeling
dizzy –

whoops!

All fall down!

Wobble's got his boots on,
walking on the wall.
Take care, Wobble Bear,
mind you don't fall!

Down you come,
Wobble Bear.

Walk, don't dash!

Now he's found a puddle so it's

splash, splash, splash!

Home through the park now,
time to go back.

Wobble does his duck-walk.

Quack, quack, quack!

Wobble Bear walks where
the other bears ride.
First he walks
the see-saw . . .

then he walks
the slide.

Walk,

. . . walk,

. . . walk,

. . . walk!

Wobble's never still . . .

till it's time to take a walk
up the wooden hill.

Wobble
squeaked
a whisper.
This is
what he
said.

'Can't walk. Too tired.
Carry me up to bed.'